Mid-Air Zillionaire

Books by Robert Elmer

www.elmerbooks.org

ASTROKIDS

#1 / *The Great Galaxy Goof*

#2 / *The Zero-G Headache*

#3 / *Wired Wonder Woof*

#4 / *Miko's Muzzy Mess*

#5 / *About-Face Space Race*

#6 / *The Cosmic Camp Caper*

#7 / *The Super-Duper Blooper*

#8 / *AstroBall Free-4-All*

#9 / *Mid-Air Zillionaire*

#10 / *Tow-Away Stowaway*

PROMISE OF ZION

#1 / *Promise Breaker*

#2 / *Peace Rebel*

#3 / *Refugee Treasure*

#4 / *Brother Enemy*

#5 / *Freedom Trap*

#6 / *True Betrayer*

ADVENTURES DOWN UNDER

#1 / *Escape to Murray River*

#2 / *Captive at Kangaroo Springs*

#3 / *Rescue at Boomerang Bend*

#4 / *Dingo Creek Challenge*

#5 / *Race to Wallaby Bay*

#6 / *Firestorm at Kookaburra Station*

#7 / *Koala Beach Outbreak*

#8 / *Panic at Emu Flat*

THE YOUNG UNDERGROUND

#1 / *A Way Through the Sea*

#2 / *Beyond the River*

#3 / *Into the Flames*

#4 / *Far From the Storm*

#5 / *Chasing the Wind*

#6 / *A Light in the Castle*

#7 / *Follow the Star*

#8 / *Touch the Sky*

ROBERT ELMER

AstroKids

9

Mid-Air Zillionaire

BETHANY BACKYARD®
www.bethanyhouse.com

Mid-Air Zillionaire
Copyright © 2002
Robert Elmer

Cover illustration by Paul Turnbaugh
Cover design by Lookout Design Group, Inc.

Published by Bethany House Publishers
A Ministry of Bethany Fellowship International
11400 Hampshire Avenue South
Bloomington, Minnesota 55438
www.bethanyhouse.com

Printed in the United States of America by
Bethany Press International, Bloomington, Minnesota 55438

Library of Congress Cataloging-in-Publication Data

Elmer, Robert.
    Mid-air zillionaire / by Robert Elmer.
        p. cm. — (Astrokids ; 9)
    Summary: Famous zillionaire Donald Zump comes to CLEO-7 looking for Miko, who runs and hides for fear of being returned to Apollo Children's Home, but the news is good: Miko has inherited an asteroid. Includes facts about asteroids and instructions for decoding a secret message.
    ISBN 0-7642-2629-0 (pbk.)
    [1. Space stations—Fiction. 2. Inheritance and succession—Fiction. 3. Christian life—Fiction. 4. Science fiction.] I. Title.
    PZ7.E4794 Mg   2002
    [Fic]—dc21

                                 2002009664

To the Scarola family.

Robert

Freckles

ROBERT ELMER is an earth-based space correspondent who writes for life-forms all over the solar system. He and his family live on a corner of the planet about ninety-three million miles from the sun. The Elmers like watching meteor showers when they go on summer vacation in Idaho, where the stars seem brighter. Or are those *meteorite* showers? *Shooting stars?* Oh dear!

Contents

$* * *$

MEET THE
AstroKids

Lamar "Buzz" Bright

Show the way, Buzz! The leader of the AstroKids always has a great plan. He also loves Jupiter ice cream.

Daphne "DeeBee" Ortiz

DeeBee's the brains of the bunch—she can build or fix almost anything. But, suffering satellites, don't tell her she's a "GEEN-ius"!

Theodore "Tag" Ortiz

Yeah, DeeBee's little brother, Tag, always tags along. Count on him to say something silly at just the wrong time. He's in orbit.

Kumiko "Miko" Sato

Everybody likes Miko the stowaway. They just don't know how she got to be a karate master, or how she knows so much about space shuttles.

Vladimir "Mir" Chekhov

So his dad's the station commander and Mir usually gets his way? Give him a break! He's trying. And whatever he did, it was probably just a joke.

1 Zump's Warning ✳ ✳ ✳

"Shhh!" My friend Buzz held a finger to his lips when he looked over his shoulder at me. I could tell he meant it. But he didn't have to warn me.

I already knew we had to be very, very quiet, so I was wearing the new anti-grav tiptoe sneakers DeeBee had given me. These were not like my old gripper shoes. Anti-grav tiptoe sneakers float two and a half centimeters off the floor. (That's about one inch, in case you were wondering.) Thanks to the sneakers, my footsteps were silent as I tiptoed right behind Buzz down hallway B–33, on the way to *CLEO–7*'s com room.

Whoops! I'm sorry! Only nine sentences into my story, and already you have two or three questions. That's my fault, not yours. Please, let me explain.

First of all, I'm Miko Sato, and *CLEO–7* is the space station where I live. The com room is where you'll find the station's sub-space communicators and things like that. And B–33 is a spot on a Bingo board game.

Ha! And you thought I was too serious to make a joke. No, this B–33 is not on a Bingo board. It's a restricted hallway.

Restricted, as in, "Are you sure it's okay we're here, Buzz?"

A station drone came buzzing down the hall, but it didn't seem to notice us. I stood still, just in case. It flew right by.

Good.

Buzz whispered back, "You worry too much, Miko. My dad lets me in here all the time. It's okay."

He didn't say if his dad had said it was okay *this* time, though. That made me worry. But did Buzz worry? Had anyone heard us get up? What if someone had followed us?

Bzzzzt-twing! The security lock did its thing and . . . *swooosh,* the door slid open to let us in. How about that. I finally remembered to take a breath. And then I followed Buzz into the dim room.

But please don't ask what we were doing there. Not yet.

"Hey, Wilson." Buzz seemed to know everyone on the station.

"Hey, Buzz. Miko." The tekky's teeth glowed orange by the light of his screen. His was one of twenty-three screens, all built into the wall. I counted every one.

He didn't ask us, "What are you two doing here at 0200 hours?" (That's two in the morning, in case you were wondering.) No, he's the one who told Buzz I'd better stop by.

"It's on screen three." Wilson nodded to a screen over by the big viewing window that faced out to the stars. "I hope the message isn't saying what I think it is."

What did he think it was? I had no idea. But this could not be good. Terrible, awful, horrible, or grim, perhaps. But not good.

And I didn't even know what the message said yet!

"Security Code Ten." Buzz whistled.

My eyebrows jumped. This *was* serious. Gulp. I was afraid to look. At the very least, this called for . . .

The Wise Space Sayings of Miko Sato, Number 01:

"It's always darkest before . . .
. . . you open your eyes."

"You have to see this, Miko," Buzz told me.

"Right." So I opened my eyes to read what it said on that bright orange screen.

SpaceMail.com—Very Urgent Message (In big letters at the top.)

security code 10 (Just like Buzz said.)

priority: ultra-high (Meaning, pretty important.)

date: April 2, 2175 (Today.)

to: CLEO–7 *Admin* ("Admin" meant space station leaders.)

from: Zump, Donald / Chairman, Apollo Children's Home Board of Directors

message: Extremely urgent that you detain runaway Miko Sato until I arrive at your station. I will take charge of her when I arrive in twenty-four hours. More details later.

So there you have it. That was all I needed to see to tell me my nightmare was coming true. They had found me! I hate to cry in front of anyone, so I didn't.

I'd rather try to get a suntan on Pluto. And that's a cold thought. I shivered.

QUESTION 01:
What's so cold about that?

ANSWER 01:
Next time you visit Pluto, get ready for about 390 degrees below zero!

"I'm sorry, Miko." Buzz patted me on the shoulder, always the good friend. But what could he say?

"What does he mean by 'runaway,' Miko?" asked Wilson. It wasn't a silly question. Only my friends knew the truth about me.

"Just that." Buzz told him for me. "She ran away and came here."

That was all Buzz said. My lip started quivering so badly I couldn't talk. I couldn't explain how my father has been on a deep-space mission since I was a baby. And I couldn't explain how I was put into the moon's Apollo Children's Home after my mother . . .

Deep sigh. After my mother . . . died.

I couldn't explain, either, what it was like to live in that place. So I won't.

"Wow." Wilson took a step back. "That's cool."

Cool wasn't the word I would have used. Cool was Pluto, and cool was *not* being chased by someone from the Apollo Children's Home.

"Do you really know Donald Zump?" Wilson looked a little like Zero-G, the dog, right before feeding time. "Donald Zump, the zillionaire? Coming here to the station? Can I meet him?"

"Thanks for telling us about the message, Wilson," Buzz said politely. "But we really have to go."

"Sure." Wilson winked at us. "I get it. And I won't tell a soul."

I did not know famous zillionaire Donald Zump. I did not know a lot of things. But I knew I had to get away from *CLEO*–7.

Fast.

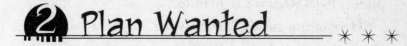 2 Plan Wanted ✳ ✳ ✳

"Miko's in big trouble," said Tag. "I mean, *gib elbuort.*"

"Stop it, Tag, this is serious." DeeBee could sure get cranked up when her little brother did his backward-talk thing.

"Gat ti pots!" he answered, still backward-talking. But no one was laughing. He looked around at four frowns and the blinking yellow warning lights on DeeBee's drone, MAC.

"Sorry." Tag held up his hands. "Just trying to make a joke."

But even Zero-G seemed to know better than to try to lighten things up just then.

"You should know, Master Tag," he said through his Mind-2-Voice box, "that six out of seven members of this group think you are not funny at the moment. Perhaps you can try again later."

"All right, all right." Buzz raised his hands to quiet everybody down. "We've got to come up with a plan. That's what we're here for."

Here meant inside the crowded cargo bay of a Y-class interlunar shuttle. We figured that the inside of the shuttle was one of the best places to meet, since nobody could hear us there.

I sat on the floor and pulled my knees to my chest.

"Look, everybody," I told them, "I am *really* sorry about this. It's all my fault, and you shouldn't have to—"

"No, no," DeeBee interrupted. Good old DeeBee. "You don't need to be sorry."

"That's right," agreed Mir. Maybe he remembered being in trouble once or twice himself. Like the time he got stuck in another shuttle, and how . . . ah, but that's another story.

QUESTION 02:

What other story are you talking about?

ANSWER 02:

The Great Galaxy Goof, remember? When Buzz first came to *CLEO*-7, and before Buzz and Mir were friends.

Mir went on, "We're going to find a way to get you out of this mess, no matter what it is."

That was sweet of him to say. But Mir didn't know how much trouble I was in!

QUESTION 03:

Okay, so how much trouble are you really in?

ANSWER 03:

Hold on, please. DeeBee is about to explain.

"Let me see if I have this straight." DeeBee rubbed her chin. "The Apollo Children's Home finally found out where Miko ran away to, and now they're sending someone to fetch her back."

"I say, did someone say *fetch*?" Zero-G picked up a gyro-ball in his mouth and wagged his tail like a rocket. "That's a very fine idea. You throw, I fetch. What do you say?"

But no one was in the mood to play gyro-catch with Zero-G.

"And they're not sending just anyone to fetch her," Buzz pointed out. "They're sending Donald Zump himself."

I checked my wrist interface. At two this morning, Mr. Zump was supposed to arrive in twenty-four hours. Now that was down to . . . twelve hours, twenty-four minutes, and twelve seconds.

"Yeah, but why?" Mir shrugged his shoulders. "Isn't he supposed to be the richest man in the solar system? Why would he be part of this?"

Yes, this was the guy who built all the famous space resorts, the huge . . .

"He owns Zump Towers." MAC knew. "Zump Resort Venus. Zumpland and Zump World. Zump, Incorporated. Zump.com. Zump Interplanet. Zump—"

"Okay, MAC." DeeBee held up her hand. "We get the idea."

Zump owned half the solar system.

"But why Zump?" I wondered out loud. "It doesn't make sense."

"Well." DeeBee scratched her head. "He's the chairman of the board of the children's home, right?"

Okay, but he was probably chairman of the board of a lot of places.

"And he loves to get his face on all the holo-vid shows, right?"

We'd all seen them. Here's Zump at the opening of a new *CLEO* space station. There's Zump on the Neta Neutron show. Wherever there was a camera, it seemed, there was Zump.

"He's probably coming here to show what a great guy he is." DeeBee had this all figured out. "You know, 'Donald Zump Rescues Poor, Lost Orphan.' That kind of thing is great for him."

Hmm. That didn't sound so bad, except for me being the poor, lost orphan. Maybe I was an orphan, but no one needed to feel sorry for me.

And I wasn't lost.

"And then, when they turn the cameras off," said Mir, "he's going to drag you back to that orphanage, where you don't have any friends and—"

"Quit it, Mir!" DeeBee waved her hands to stop him. "We don't want to give Miko nightmares."

Too late.

"I know!" Tag's face lit up, as if he had just invented time travel. "What if he's not really being sent by the Apollo Children's Home, and he's coming here to give us a big prize?"

No one said anything. I listened to MAC's memory whirring.

"Or not." Tag shrugged.

"It was a nice thought," I told him.

"This is all very interesting," Buzz finally said. "But we do need a plan. A real plan." Leave it to Buzz to get us back on track. He was supposed to be the leader of us AstroKids, after all.

A real plan would be nice. My only plan was to borrow this shuttle and fly it straight to the outer solar system. Maybe I should have done that in the first place, before coming to *CLEO-7* and making all these friends. Now, I was as much fun for them as a wobbly asteroid about to crash into the station.

In other words, I was trouble. And that's just what I told them.

"Phooey," said DeeBee. "We stick together like a rope."

"Pardon me?" Mine probably wasn't the only confused face.

"You know. A cord of three strands is not easily broken. Or five strands, or seven, for that matter."

I knew that was supposed to mean something. I just wasn't sure what.

"It's in the Bible," she said with a shrug. "It means that friends stick together."

"Oh." I didn't want to hurt her feelings, but how would that help? "Well, thank you for wanting to help me and everything. But maybe it would be better if I just left."

DeeBee: "YG2BK!" (Which stands for, "You've Got To Be Kidding.")

Buzz: "Way wrong!"

Tag: "No way!"

Mir: "Nyet!"

MAC: "Your idea is not logical."

Zero-G: "Who would play gyro-catch with me?"

Me: "Oh-oh. Did you feel that?"

They had to. A rumbly *whrrrrr* started to shake the floor beneath our feet. And that could only mean one thing.

Oh dear. Our shuttle was going to take off!

Choco-Jupiter
3 Shake-Up ✳ ✳ ✳

Ten, nine . . .

"We've got to get out of here!" yelled Buzz as he headed for the door.

eight, seven . . .

For a moment, I thought maybe my prayers had been answered. I was getting away *and* we were all together. This was perfect, right?

six, five . . .

Wrong. We would stick together, yes. But this flight was going straight to the moon. That was the *last* place I wanted to go. We would have to deshuttle now!

"What's the problem, Miko?" DeeBee wanted to know.

I was trying to move, but I couldn't.

"How do you turn off these anti-grav tiptoe sneakers?" I asked.

four, three . . .

This was not a good time for me to be running in place and not moving!

two, one . . .

"Come on, girl!" DeeBee grabbed my hand and dragged me out the shuttle door.

Waaa-waaa-waaa! An alarm sounded, and a computerized woman's voice blared over the shuttle hangar 02 sound system.

"Security field breach!" said the voice. "Abort take-off!"

Hiiiiisssss . . . The shuttle shut itself off in a whoosh of servo-steam.

"We're very sorry!" I told the pilot who met us at the door to the shuttle hangar. He didn't smile and nod back at me like captains usually do when you get off their shuttle.

"This way!" Mir thought we should hide as far away from the hub of *CLEO–7* as we could.

"No, this way!" DeeBee had a different idea.

So did Buzz.

In the end, we did what we AstroKids usually did. We panicked.

"In here!" I told them. I ducked inside a little

door I had never seen before. What do you think that little circle with the line through it means?

QUESTION 04:

What does it mean?

ANSWER 04:

You know. The "don't" circle? As in, DO NOT ENTER?

"Don't breathe," Buzz commanded us once we were all inside. Of course, MAC was the only one who could obey.

Tag started to giggle, and DeeBee clamped her hand over his mouth.

"Shh!" she told him.

I heard someone running by in the hallway. Was the person looking for me?

I thought for a minute about adjusting my anti-grav sneakers then. Until I saw that everyone else was floating, too.

"Welcome to weightless compartment J–83," announced Buzz softly.

QUESTION 05:

Weightless? Why is the compartment weight-less?

ANSWER 05:

Remember that the station is shaped like a giant spinning hamburger? There's not much gravity in the middle by the shuttle hangars.

So for now this was my hideout. Home, sweet home.

"You stay in here for now, Miko," said Buzz, "until we figure out what to do."

I nodded. If I couldn't borrow a shuttle and escape to Pluto, I supposed I could float around for a while in a closet full of pipes and wires. After all, I was pretty good at hiding.

"Are you going to be all right?" Mir asked.

Well, I would have to be.

DeeBee made me feel a little better. "FYI," she said, "we'll come check on you every couple of hours."

That would be good.

Meanwhile, Mir's stomach rumbled.

"Well, time to eat," he said. Even fear couldn't make him forget food.

"You have to promise you aren't going to forget me in here," I told them.

Perhaps I should not have worried. But when the door went *fttt* and *click* behind them, well, you can guess how alone I felt. I looked around at my little hiding place: six meters deep, three meters wide, three meters tall. A little cozy for long-term living.

The pipes on the walls made hissing and rumbling noises. That was okay. At least no one would hear me sniffling. DeeBee would call it *blubbering*.

So there I was, blubbering in my hiding place, drifting around, when the door went *click* and *fttt* again.

Quick! Hide! I squeezed behind a couple of pipes in the ceiling. But all anyone would have to do is look up to see me.

"What are you doing up there, Miko?" Tag smiled up at me and held out a blue cup. "I brought you a choco-Jupiter shake to cheer you up."

"A choco-Jupiter shake?" My favorite. "That was very sweet of—"

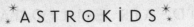

I am sure Tag didn't mean it. He must have forgotten I was in a weightless closet. And you know what happens to a creamy choco-Jupiter shake in a weightless room.

A shake without a lid on the cup.

To be fair, I should tell you that everyone else came to help us clean up. But if you've ever tried to mop up globs of floating choco-Jupiter shake, you know how un-fun that can be.

Only Mir looked happy. He drifted around the room with his mouth open, sort of like a human vacuum cleaner.

"Hey, this works pretty good," he told us.

I have to confess I was pretty glad Buzz double-locked the door behind them. Especially after I saw him talking with DeeBee in a low voice over in the corner of my hideout.

"What are they saying, MAC?" I asked the drone. Maybe that was sneaky, but I knew MAC could hear. And that he would tell me.

"Oh, they do not want you to worry, Miko."

"Too late for that! Just tell me, MAC. Please?"

"Well, the Interstar Police are looking for you, and

everyone on the station is searching for you."

I groaned. Choco-Jupiter shake or no choco-Jupiter shake, this runaway thing was going from bad to worse.

Miko Protection Force

4

***

You know it's always good to be polite. So I smiled a few hours later when DeeBee gave me a box.

"For me?"

DeeBee nodded.

"Thank you very much," I told her. "But—"

"Aren't you going to open it?" asked Mir.

"Let's see it," added Buzz.

Well, the boys were hardly going to give me a chance to open it myself. So I lifted the lid and peeked inside.

"Ohhhh." I tried to feel excited, but I have to be honest. Hiding in weightless compartment J-83 for hours and hours was starting to give me the creeps. And a present from DeeBee was nice, but—

"Come on," said DeeBee. Her voice went up a notch. "Try it on."

Well, okay. But how? Did the strap go around my

head, or my ankle? And what was the round silver yo-yo in the middle of the belt supposed to do? Transport me to the outer system? That would be nice.

"It's a . . ." I wasn't sure if I was supposed to know what this was. I didn't want to be rude, but I didn't have a clue.

DeeBee pulled it out of the box for me. "It's the MPF emitter I've been working on. My dad had some spare parts he let me have."

"Cool." I held the belt up to my arm. "Thanks again."

"Here. It goes around your waist, silly." DeeBee quickly strapped it into position. The silver yo-yo faced forward, like an overgrown moon rodeo belt buckle. Maybe that was what DeeBee called the "emitter."

She looked at me with a grin. "You still don't know what this is, do you?"

"Of course I do. It's an MPF. Maybe I've always needed one."

Everybody laughed.

"Okay," I admitted. "I give up. I don't know what this thing is. It looks cool, but I don't know what it is."

QUESTION 06:

I give up, too. MPF stands for what?

ANSWER 06:

I think we'll need DeeBee to explain.

"MPF stands for Macro Protection Force," she told us. "It puts a clear protector bubble field all around you."

"So no one from the Apollo Children's Home can grab you!" Mir seemed to think this was a great idea, too.

"It's perfect." Buzz agreed with him.

DeeBee showed me the easy-to-flip switch on the side, the one that powered up the force field. But, she told me about five times, it was only for an emergency.

That was fine with me. I was afraid to tell her I didn't think I would ever turn it on. I did not want to hurt her feelings. It *was* a great idea, but I didn't want to be part of an experiment.

"*We're* the Miko Protection Force," yelled Tag, and he went into a wobbly-looking karate position. "We'll protect you."

Tag was always ready to try a karate kick.

QUESTION 07:

Hold it, hold it. There's another MPF?

ANSWER 07:

Right. The MACRO Protection Force is the
gadget, but the MIKO Protection Force is
Tag's way of protecting me. Sorry to confuse
you.

"Hiiii-YAA!" yelled Tag. He was so far off it
wasn't funny.

I reached out for his foot as he sailed by.

"Here, you're going to hurt yourself," I told him
when I grabbed his ankle. "You need to do it the
right way."

"Why don't you show me? You're the expert."

"Well . . ."

"You can show all of us. We'll be your body-
guards, plus you have DeeBee's MPF belt. Then
you'll *really* be safe."

Maybe for now. But no one was talking about how
long I would be able to hide like this.

"Please show me?" Tag wasn't giving up.

I don't know how I let him sweet-talk me into it.

But a few minutes later, I had them all lined up, showing them basic karate kicks and moves. I didn't want them to hurt themselves doing it the wrong way.

"Left foot, KICK!" I said. This was as close as I got to being a drill sergeant.

"Hiiii-YAAAA!" they all yelled back. You should have seen them. Even Zero-G gave it a shot.

"Right foot, KICK!"

"Waaaa-HIIII!"

Maybe we didn't need to worry about hiding in weightless compartment J–83 anymore. With all the noise we were making, someone was going to find us soon.

"Once more!" Still, I was starting to get into this. Maybe a Miko Protection Force wasn't such a bad idea after all. But as for DeeBee's belt, well, I have to be honest: Would *you* wear something like that?

Okay, maybe you would. I know the boys would have. They thought everything was cool, especially learning a few karate moves.

"Watch out!" cried Tag. "I'm an MPF!"

Of course he was. But he forgot we were all weightless in my hiding place. So Tag came at me full speed, legs out and hands flying.

I still don't know quite how it happened. As best I can remember, Tag planted his foot in my stomach, and I know he didn't mean to hurt me. He was just playing around. He surely didn't mean to power up the MPF belt.

It was an accident.

"Whoops." Maybe Tag felt his heel brush against the emergency switch.

But everyone had to hear the loud crackle and hum of the belt coming on. And everyone had to see my arms and legs shoot straight out, sending poor Tag flying across the room as if he had been launched from the moon.

"Whoaaaaa!" he cried as he smashed first into Buzz, then Mir. They all three crumpled into the far wall by the door.

What was happening here?

Airsick Bag, 5 Anyone?

★ ★ ★

If you've been following the action, you know that the MPF was working great. Actually, it was working a little too great.

"Oh!" I tried to wave my hands, but they were sticking straight out. By this, I mean *straight* out and right in the middle of the force field.

"Ha-ha!" Mir couldn't help laughing. "You look like you're the pit in the middle of a clear jelly ball, Miko. Way too funny."

Well, I am sorry to say this was *not* funny. It was not amusing, humorous, comical, or laughable. It was not anything like that. I felt like an out-of-control satellite!

"You look like . . ." Tag had to take another breath, he was giggling so hard. "You look like an out-of-control satellite, Miko."

I believe I just said that.

"How do you keep your arms and legs out so straight?" Mir wanted to know.

I wanted an answer to that, too.

"I really can't help it." That's about all I could tell them.

Buzz wiped the smile from his face and came closer. "I'll turn it off."

Thank you, Buzz. He was the only gentleman in the bunch. But I'm afraid he didn't help much. Because when he got about a meter away, he just bounced off.

"That's odd." He lowered his head and tried again.

Doinnnng . . . The air twinkled where Buzz ran into the MPF bubble, and you could sort of see where the force field was by the quivering, Jell-O-like look of the air around me. But he couldn't get any closer.

"Sorry, Miko." He had tried his best, I know.

I felt like I was the yolk of an egg. I couldn't even lower my hands to turn the silly thing off.

(Whoops! Please don't tell DeeBee I said her invention was "silly." I would not want to be rude.)

"Well, maybe it needs a little tweaking." DeeBee pulled out a black remote control.

"Tweaking!" Mir's shoulders were shaking by this time.

"Is that what I think it is?" I asked. Good old DeeBee! She'd thought of everything.

"Yeah, don't worry." She smiled and pointed the remote at me. "Those boys can laugh all they want. But I've got you covered. All I do is press this button, and . . ."

I was hoping DeeBee's remote would switch off the MPF. Maybe you were hoping the same thing.

"Suffering satellites!" She fiddled with a thumb control. "You're disappearing. Maybe the polarity is wrong."

Disappearing? What next? Now the outside shell of the MPF really sparked every time it hit something.

Or someone.

"Pardon me!" I said.

Zero-G spun away, paws over tail.

"Excuse me!"

Mir flew backward.

"Oh dear!"

"Where are you, Miko?" yelled Buzz.

This was not good. My MPF bubble wasn't shutting down. Not at all. In fact, it had started bouncing around that little room without stopping. And every time it hit the wall or bounced into someone, it bounced back even faster.

Boing.

"Sorry!"

Boing-boing.

"I didn't mean to push you around."

Boing-boing-boing.

Don't forget that I was planted in the middle of this awful jelly-like bouncing ball. And my poor stomach was sending me upset messages.

A Dizzying Chat with Miko Sato's... Stomach

Miko's stomach: Hey! What's going on out there?

Miko: I'm very sorry, but—

Miko's stomach: No excuses, missy. The ride stops now, or else!

Miko: My apologies. I don't want you to get upset.

Miko's stomach: Upset? You haven't *seen* upset!

And so on. I'm afraid I could not tell my stomach to settle down any more than I could stop the MPF from bouncing all over. What now?

Well, the AstroKids did the only thing they could.

"Let's get out of here!" yelled Buzz.

Boing-boing . . .

"Unlock the door!" shouted Mir.

Bounce! *Smack!*

"Abandon ship!" cried Tag, waving his arms.

But wouldn't you know it? DeeBee had barely jumped out into the hallway after the others when my lovely MPF bubble aimed straight for her backside.

"Gangway! I mean, pardon me, please!" I tried to warn her, but I could only watch as the MPF hit the doorway straight on. It hung there for just a second, popped through, picked up even more speed, and . . .

"DEEBEEEE!" I yelled.

"Whaaaa?" she yelled back.

Well, a lot of good that did. Now poor DeeBee Ortiz was plastered to the outside of my MPF bubble like a fly on a see-through asteroid. Now you could see its globe shape by the way she wrapped her arms and legs around it. We were bouncing down the hall—fast!

"Hold on!" I told her.

Oh dear. What had we done?

Come to think of it, this was just like a game of space bowl. Except instead of pins at the end of the lane, we had three AstroKids, running for their lives. Not to mention Zero-G, who had just turned the corner at the end of the hallway.

Plus, I forgot to mention the little group of adults who had just turned the corner, strolling toward us.

FOUR adults who watched . . .

THREE boys run by . . .

TWO steps ahead of a girl flying straight at them, stuck on the front end of . . .

ONE big, sparkling ball of energy.

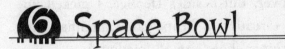

6 Space Bowl

Now, maybe you are wondering what happened to Donald Zump. Wasn't the richest man in the solar system supposed to be coming to *CLEO-7*, you ask? Shouldn't he be landing on the station to find the poor, lost orphan and bring her back to the Apollo Children's Home?

If that's what you're wondering, well, you have a fine memory. And if you had been stuck inside a big see-through MPF force-field ball zipping down hallway 33-E, you might have heard and seen the same things I did.

"This way, Mr. Zump," one man said.

"We'll find her for you, Mr. Zump," another said.

"WARNING!" alerted a personal drone.

Or something like that. It all happened so fast, you understand.

BAAAM! ZNORT! SPRACKLE! OOOF!

My MPF bounced around the corner and down the hall. I cannot tell you what happened to the poor people I ran over. But besides DeeBee, I picked up one personal e-reader, a drone com antenna, and somebody's gripper shoe (size 12, medium).

And still we rumbled down the hall and around another corner, right behind the boys.

Aren't they tired yet?

Boinga-boinga. We bounced from wall to wall.

And then I thought of something.

"Grab them, DeeBee!" I yelled. It seemed like a good idea.

What else could DeeBee do? Just before we would have flattened Buzz, Mir, and Tag, she grabbed the nearest arms and held on. I don't know how she managed to come up with all three of them. Now we could all see what we had to do.

"Landing gear, everybody!" I had a picture in my mind of my MPF squashing them against the far wall. Double ouch! It might have been just a big blob of energy, but it was trucking right along.

DeeBee and the boys stretched out their legs. And so there we were, a big ball with eight legs held out to stop us.

Kind of like a giant spider, I suppose.

You would have been proud of them. Because when we hit the wall, I could feel their legs bend.

Instead of bouncing back again the other direction, the ball sort of died right there. Which was good.

Houston, the Macro Protection Force has landed.

Well, almost. The energy field blinked a couple of times, and I thought maybe I was free. But not so fast. Remember the four adults we bowled over?

I could hear them coming down the hall, and they didn't sound happy.

"Uh-oh." Buzz looked for a way out as the MPF finally flickered and dumped me on the floor.

"Owf!"

Gravity, meet Miko Sato. Miko, meet gravity. The boys picked me up, and we scooted through a side door to safety.

At least for the moment. I still felt like a sack of spare shuttle parts as we zipped down the hall—right, then left, then down hallway 21-C, and finally into DeeBee's workshop, where we all fell on the floor.

"Oh, boy!" gasped Tag.

"I haven't run that fast since . . ." Buzz didn't know.

My legs felt like double-microwaved noodles.

A Shakey Chat with Miko Sato's . . . Legs

Miko's legs: We're on strike, you know.

Miko: I am sorry to hear that. I didn't mean to startle you, back in the hallway.

Miko's legs: Startle us? First, we're weightless, then we're not, then, *bam*! Now you want us to carry your weight again, just like that? Dream on!

"Well, look at the bright side." DeeBee had already started taking the MPF yo-yo emitter disk apart.

I was still sitting on the shop floor, gasping.

Bright side?

"You were invisible inside the MPF." She sounded excited about it. "Nobody could see you."

"Is that all?" I tried to sound polite.

"And super-powering the MPF also ran down the battery a lot quicker."

She tossed a power disk to the side and slipped in a new one.

"Oh." I rubbed my arms, which still felt stiff from being stuck inside the MPF. "I suppose that *is* good news."

"Right." DeeBee then punched a bunch of numbers into her remote control, pointed it at the belt buckle emitter, and nodded. "Now that I have it reprogrammed, it's going to work just fine."

"Oh no!" I put up my hands. "I mean, I think I've had enough of being in the middle of an MPF for one day. If you don't mind, that is."

"Hey, don't worry." DeeBee smiled and strapped the emitter back around my waist. "It's totally new. Totally different."

Another Heart-to-Heart Chat with Miko Sato's . . . Stomach

Miko's stomach: Now, wait just a minute. You're not going to spin me around again, are you?

Miko: I would hope not to.

Miko's stomach: Hope-schmope! I can't take it anymore!

"Trust me, Miko. This is nothing like the old MPF."

Well, it sure *looked* the same. Suddenly Mir and Buzz stood by the door, looking like Space Olympic runners ready to go. "On your mark, get set . . ." Who peeled them off the floor so quickly?

"So what does it do now?" Tag took a baby step closer. But maybe he shouldn't have. Everyone could hear the yo-yo emitter sending out a high-pitched hum.

Oh dear!

The Mighty Face-Lifter

7   * * *

I guess DeeBee wasn't about to give up.

"You aren't scared, are you?" She turned to MAC with her remote control. "It's just warming up."

MAC edged toward the door with the boys, and his yellow warning lights started blinking.

Remember, now: I'm the one wearing the yo-yo emitter thing. And DeeBee is the one wearing a grin. To me, that's something to worry about.

"You are holding a phase three cellular data-beta scanner," MAC finally answered. "Why should I be afraid of that?"

"There, see?" DeeBee turned and smiled at the rest of us. "It's just an itty-bitty phase three cellular data-beta scanner. Here, I'll show you how it works."

DeeBee held her remote control thingy right up next to MAC's face, and we could see green light beams wash across him.

"Does it hurt?" she asked.

"No pain."

Wait a minute. Did drones even feel pain?

Next, she pointed her scanner at my yo-yo belt buckle, waited for a few seconds, and reached over to power up my switch.

"Not again!" I pulled back.

"Will you relax?" She held me by the shoulder. "I promise, no MPF this time."

"No invisible force fields?" I wanted to make double sure.

"Cross my heart. Now watch."

She flipped the switch, and I heard a whooshing sound around my face, a flush of power that made my hair stand up.

Everyone stared at me and then burst out laughing.

"What's so funny?" I asked.

DeeBee giggled. Mir chuckled. Even Buzz rolled on the floor.

"Say something else," DeeBee held the sides of her smile to keep from breaking up.

"A, B, C. Testing, testing. One, two, three, four . . ."

That sent them all rolling with laughter.

"So now I'm a comedian?"

More laughs.

Zero-G came up to sniff.

"The leg smells like Miss Miko," he said, and then he looked up at me. "But the face is the drone's."

Oh. Now I got it.

"So it's like a mask?" I asked DeeBee.

"Even better. It's a 3-D holo-mask that covers your face perfectly. Here. I can scan anybody, and the Face-Lifter lifts their face and puts it on yours."

"Here, let me try!" Tag was the first in line, so I unbuckled the Face-Lifter belt for him to wear.

"Please, be my guest." Take it!

And for the next hour, everybody else tried it out, too. Buzz wore Mir's head. Mir put on Buzz's. DeeBee wore my face. Everyone thought that was a scream. But what was this thing really good for?

"Okay, everybody." DeeBee finally raised her hands. "Enough fun and games. The Face-Lifter goes back to Miko now."

So soon?

"Oh, that's okay," I told them. "I'll share."

"Nope. It's for you." DeeBee fixed the belt back

on me and flipped on the power once again.

Whoosh. Zip. Crackle. This time I could tell I was wearing someone else's holo-face. DeeBee's, I think.

"So, here's the plan," DeeBee said. "Now Miko can walk around without having to hide, because she looks just like me."

"Only, you two can't be in the same place." Mir started to laugh again. "Because if you are—"

Yes, that is what I was afraid would happen, too.

"But what if someone asks us where Miko is?" Tag wanted to know. "We can't lie, can we?"

"No." Buzz frowned and rubbed his chin. "We'll think of something."

Yes, of course we would. And here was a good example: Five minutes later, when the door buzzer went *deeeep-deeeep!*

"I'm leaving!" I told them. When Buzz opened the door, I was the first one out. Right into the four people I'd run into earlier!

"Pardon me." I tried to smile, but I was shaking too much. The tall man in the middle of the group stared right at me but moved to the side. His expensive gray suit looked a little rumpled. But there was no doubt about it.

Donald Zump!

"Have we met?" he asked me. He turned his head to the side the way dogs sometimes do when they're listening to something. Zero-G does it all the time.

A Pointed Chat with Miko Sato's ... Knees

Miko: Please don't fail me now!

Miko's knees: Sorry. *Knock-knock*. We seem to be stuck.

Miko: Just relax and stop knocking into each other. Take a deep breath.

Miko's knees: Breath? What's that?

"No. I don't think we've met." I swallowed hard and finally got my legs to move backward.

"Hmm." Donald Zump turned to the others. His assistant held up a pocket holo-projector, and a 3-D picture of me popped up. Oh dear! What a terrible picture! But it was me.

"We're looking for this girl," said Zump's assistant. "We think she may be hiding here somewhere. It's very important that we find her. In fact, we have a big reward."

"How big?" asked Mir.

"Mir!" Buzz scolded him.

I could not listen anymore. I backed away and hurried down the hall.

The question now: How long could I hide behind DeeBee's Face-Lifter?

8 Search for Miko ✳ ✳ ✳

This wasn't so hard. It wasn't so bad. I could pretend I was DeeBee.

"Hey, DeeBee!" a tekky smiled and waved at me as I sat down to eat in the dining hall that evening. "How's it going?"

"Er, great." I tried to think of something DeeBee would say. "That is, I mean, I could be wrong, ICBW, I mean, but . . . perfectamundo!"

There. That was DeeBee-speak, wasn't it?

The tekky looked at me kind of funny.

"Where are your friends?" he asked.

Good question. I had managed to keep out of their way all evening.

A Quiet Chat with Miko Sato's . . . Lips

Miko's lips: So, you want us to say something clever?

Miko: I don't know if "clever" is the right word.

Miko's lips: What about something true, then?

Oh dear. Oh my. This was worrisome. I took a big swallow of milk and started to choke.

Ahem. HACK-HACK!

No, this was not part of the act.

"Hey there." My tekky friend slapped me square on the back. I could tell he meant well. "You okay, DeeBee?"

"Sure." *Hack-hack*. "I'm just . . ."

I'm just having a heart attack, because guess who just walked in the door?

Yes. It was DeeBee. Her dad was holding her arm, the way teachers do when they're marching someone to the principal's office, or the way parents do when they are just about to turn you over to the authorities to spend the rest of your life in prison. MAC floated along behind her. Or rather, he dragged along. Next came her mom, walking with that kind of walk you see at funerals. And next to her marched a man that looked a lot like Mr. Donald Zump, with his assistants buzzing all around him.

I can tell you one thing for sure: They did not

look like happy campers.

So I did what any brave space pioneer would do.

"What are you doing under the table, DeeBee?" the tekky asked.

"Er . . ." I tried to crawl to the other side. Maybe I could get out of there. I'd try a garbage chute, anything. Maybe they hadn't seen me yet. "I'm not feeling well."

Actually, that was very true. I held my head to keep it from spinning. The feeling of creepy-crawlies all over my face made me want to scratch all over. I peeked out from the other side of the table to see where the real DeeBee had gone.

"Oh, hi there." I looked straight into DeeBee's face when she bent down to see me.

And then it happened.

SPACKLE! SPARKLE! ZAT!

Double ouch! Triple ouch! My head felt terrible now. Hiding under the table was no good. But when I climbed out, all the adults looked at me as if I had some kind of deep-space virus. Their eyes went big, and they each took a step back. Even Mr. Donald Zump looked as if he wanted to be somewhere else.

And, yes, they were all staring at me!

"What's going on, DeeBee?" I whispered. When I looked at my reflection in a shiny spot on MAC's side, I nearly fell over backward.

You should have seen it.

My hair looked like Buzz's, very dark and curly. Tag calls it frizzy. I like it very much, only not on my head.

The eyes belonged to Mir, I think—light blue and twinkling. Only sometimes they switched to MAC's three electronic eyes, on little eye stalks. That was a cute touch. But where had the nose and mouth come from?

"We shouldn't have scanned Zero-G," whispered DeeBee, shaking her head.

She was right. The color of the fur was all wrong.

"Did I tell you," she went on, "that you're not supposed to drink anything when you've got the Face-Lifter powered up?"

I did not remember her saying anything like that. Not that it mattered anymore.

DeeBee looked down. "It shorts out the system."

As in *poof!* Sparks fly, power zaps, people jump. And that is exactly what happened a second later. Or rather . . .

Ka-FOOO-eey! Fickle-zickle . . . ZAPOLA!

I have seen laser light shows and fireworks before, back when I lived on the moon. This was almost as good. But when it was done, what was left?

Just me. Me wearing my real face. No more Face-Lifter.

The whooshing sound was gone, and a bit of curling gray smoke rose from the yo-yo-shaped silver Face-Lifter control. Where my family comes from, this is called losing face.

"Well, it was a nice idea," I told DeeBee. I had to be polite with everyone staring at me.

"Miss Miko Sato, I presume?" The richest man in the solar system reached out to shake my hand. He looked different than I remembered him from holovids. But I was pretty sure it was him. "It's an honor to finally meet you."

Donald Zump was smiling.

Houston, we have a problem.

⑨ Just Sign Here ✳ ✳ ✳

So the gig was up. The act was over. As Buzz would say, we were toast.

Burnt toast.

No more hiding. No more running. No more karate kicks and Miko Protection Forces. I reached down and switched off the broken Face-Lifter. Whew! No more Face-Lifters, either. Please don't tell DeeBee, but I thought perhaps her invention needed more work.

"I am so pleased we finally caught up with you." Mr. Zump pumped my hand up and down. "We ran into a little, er . . . trouble on the way."

That was true, if "trouble" meant being bowled over by a big MPF ball.

"I am very sorry," I began, and I kept my eyes pointed at the floor. "We did not mean to—"

"What Miss Sato is trying to say . . ." DeeBee's dad cut in. "Is, well, she's glad you finally found her. Isn't that right, Miko?"

If I nodded, I would be lying. If I looked up, they would see the tears in my eyes. No, I was not glad. I would say nothing.

"The poor dear." DeeBee's mom came to the rescue. "She's been through so much."

"Of course she has." Even Mr. Zump's voice was different in person than it was on the holo-vid newscasts. "Ever since she ran away from the Apollo Children's Home."

He pointed to the screen on the e-reader one of his stony-faced assistants gave him.

"And I must say, it adds up."

What was that?

He began to read. "Cost for extra search teams, $122,400."

Uh-oh.

"Cost for launching search shuttle, $343,000."

I had not thought of that.

"Cost for overtime administration, $129,212."

I was not exactly sure what that was.

"Cost for private investigator to locate runaway, $498,003."

I wondered where the three extra dollars came from.

"We can pay it all back," DeeBee blurted out. "Miko belongs here with us. My parents want to adopt her."

Bless her heart. But her father held her back while Mr. Zump smiled and punched a couple of buttons on his e-reader.

"So, the total for your escape adventure comes to . . . $1,092,615."

He smiled and shook his head. "You've become an expensive young lady, Miss Sato."

Face it, I told myself. *My life is over.*

I would have to go back to the Apollo Children's Home. I do not want to even think about how lonely I would be there. You can't imagine what it was like.

Even worse, I would probably have to work a hundred years to pay back all that money.

"I am very sorry to have caused you all that trouble," I whispered. Mr. Zump leaned forward to hear me. "I did not mean to . . ."

"Of course you didn't." He was smiling again

now. "But I have a proposal for you that will take care of everything."

Everything? This idea of Mr. Zump's would be worth all $1,092,615?

"Yes, you heard me right." Another assistant gave him still another e-reader. Mr. Zump powered up the bright screen with a touch of his hand and served it up to us like a fine dinner. "It's all very simple, really."

Everyone gathered around to read the screen. I could make out the words "inheritance" and my name, but everything else was full of words like "whereby" and "heretofore" and "thereupon."

Even DeeBee's dad scratched his head as he read it.

"I'm not quite sure, Miko, but it looks as if you've inherited something." He turned to me. "Did you know you were this person's great-great fourth cousin, three times removed?"

"I don't think so." I tried to think. I didn't know *any* of my relatives, much less a great-great fourth-removed someone.

What was this? Why was my name on it? I leaned closer to MAC. His three eyes scanned the document, back and forth. If anyone could make sense of it, MAC could. But Mr. Zump leaned closer, and his hand covered the bottom part of the reader.

"It is a planet," reported MAC. "Miko, you have inherited a planet."

"A worthless asteroid," said Mr. Zump. "Asteroid A–222. Just sign here, and we'll call it even. You owe us nothing, and you can stay here with your, er, friends."

"That sounds wonderfully generous, Mr. Zump," said DeeBee's mom.

"More than generous, Mr. Zump," added her dad.

"Suffering satellites!" DeeBee couldn't believe it. "All that for a junk asteroid?"

"Can I have your autograph, Mr. Zump?" Tag asked.

I thought and thought. This did not make sense to me. And while I thought and thought, MAC tugged and tugged on my sleeve.

"Please. Later, MAC," I told him.

"What do you say, Miss Sato?" Mr. Zump held out a blank e-reader and a stylus to sign it. "All you need to do is sign right here, and I'll be on my way.

I'll have my company, Zump Interplanetary, take care of all the details."

He stood there, waiting.

"Sign it, Miko!" said DeeBee. Maybe she was right, but . . .

"Pardon me, but could I please ask you something?" I didn't want to upset anyone. I just had to know.

"Anything, of course." But I noticed Mr. Zump's hand was shaking just a bit.

"Well, if Asteroid A–222 is as worthless as you say, and I'm sure you're right, why does Zump Interplanetary want it?"

"Ah, a simple question with a simple answer." He turned to Assistant Number One. "What's the simple answer?"

While Assistant Number One told us how they would mine for funny-sounding minerals like trimagnesium and disulphate, MAC tugged on my sleeve again. I tried to ignore him, because I wanted to understand what Assistant Number One was talking about. But then MAC floated up close to my head and whispered in my ear.

"Do not sign, Miss Miko!" he hissed. I think he meant it.

"What? Why not?"

"In private." He pulled me away from the group. "Where no one else can hear."

10 Off Course ✳ ✳ ✳

"Why shouldn't I sign?" I whispered to MAC. "It's just an old asteroid."

"Look." MAC showed me a small holo-projection of a newscaster.

"In other news, work has just been completed on an expensive new hotel and restaurant center on Asteroid A-222, one of the most beautiful stops on Interstar Route Y-55 . . ."

"Can I help you with something?" Mr. Zump called to us from across the room. He was still holding his e-reader and stylus.

I smiled and waved.

"What does this mean?" I asked MAC. I was confused.

"I do not have enough data to know for sure." MAC's bubble drive bubbled. "But it looks as if Asteroid A-222 may be more valuable than Mr. Zump would like you to believe."

"How much more?"

"Not enough data. But millions more. Maybe billions more."

"You mean he's trying to cheat me?"

"Hmmm," MAC hummed. "I will look for more information. But you must see for yourself."

I took a deep breath. This would not be easy. But I said a prayer for courage. Then I took MAC's hand and marched back to the others.

"I have decided what I will do," I told them.

"Splendid." Mr. Zump beamed even wider and held out his e-reader and stylus. "Now, if you'll just sign here."

"I'm not going to sign."

Mr. Zump froze as if someone had just opened up a window on the dark side of the station. Believe me, it's a little brisk out there.

QUESTION 08:

How cold would it be?

ANSWER 08:

Try 250 degrees below zero on the shady side. About as cold as Mr. Zump's stare, just then.

"You're *not* going to sign?" He couldn't believe it.

"I don't want to cause problems." I held my breath. "But I need to see A–222 first. Then maybe I will sign."

Mr. Zump closed his eyes and tightened his fists. For a moment, I thought he was going to cry, the way his bottom lip started to twitch. But he nodded when Assistant Number One leaned over and whispered something in his ear.

"Well, of course you can see the asteroid." He took a deep breath and smiled again. "You can ride with us. We'll make a picnic out of it and be right back."

I was not sure what kind of a picnic this would be. And I was a little worried forty minutes later, when I said good-bye to everybody before stepping onto Donald Zump's huge shuttle. DeeBee's parents weren't so sure about this, either, but Zump promised to take good care of me.

"Whoop-whoo!" Tag had to lean his head back to see the whole ship at once. "I wonder how that shuttle fit in the hangar. It's huge-*mongous*!"

I was wondering more than that. But now I needed to do what I had decided. I had to go through with it. And believe me on this one: I wondered a hundred times why I hadn't just signed where Mr. Zump had asked me to sign. That would have been the end of it.

"You're doing the right thing," Buzz told me as we said good-bye. I guess coming from him, I knew it was true. He gave me a quick hug.

DeeBee's hug wasn't so quick, since she had something to tell me.

"Don't look now, but I put something extra in Mom's food basket for you."

"Thanks, DeeBee." I dabbed at my eye. "You didn't need to—"

"Don't thank me. Just listen: It's the MPF remote control."

I froze up. Please, not again! Not the MPF!

"Look, don't worry," she whispered. "I did some quick work on it. I fixed the power problem. And you can switch back and forth now between the MPF and the Face-Lifter. I clipped the emitter onto MAC."

"Why MAC?"

DeeBee looked around to make sure no one could hear us.

"I just thought you could use some company."

"But . . . where is he?"

DeeBee nodded to an open cargo door where a couple of men were loading supplies.

"He'll find you."

And then she turned away, but she left something in my hand. A piece of string? But when I looked closer, I saw the strands, wound around each other.

Five strands.

"All right!" hollered Mr. Zump. "If we're going to see A–222 and be back here before tomorrow, we'd best be off."

I tucked the string into my pocket, picked up my food basket, and did as I was told. But all through the launch, I couldn't help worrying.

Am I really coming back?

And I wondered what MAC was up to, hiding away inside the shuttle. But I didn't have long to think about it.

Actually, I'll skip over the next part: Getting into the shuttle, strapping into our seats, taking off . . . Everything happened the way it should have. Everything was routine. Normal. At least, that's what I thought until twenty minutes later, when I had just shut the bathroom door behind me.

"Eek!" I nearly backed through the closed door.

"What are you doing here, MAC?"

"Shh!" MAC put a finger up to his mouth. "This is the only place we can talk in secret."

"But what's so secret?" I still didn't get it.

"You are in danger, Miss Miko."

I gulped.

"They are not taking you to Asteroid A–222, and they are not taking you back to the station."

Now *there* was an ion blast to the chest!

"How do you know?" I squeaked.

MAC had only to replay a fuzzy 3-D holo-snapshot of what he had seen. And there they were: a tiny Donald Zump and Assistant Number One, talking in low voices. The snapshot looked as if it had been taken just a few moments before.

Assistant Number One: "Course laid in for the asteroid field, sir. Which one do you want to show her?"

Zump (laughing): "Doesn't matter to me, as long as she thinks it's A–222."

Assistant Number One: "Very good, sir. She signs the will over to you, and . . ."

Zump: "And it's straight back to the Apollo Children's Home for Miss Miko Sato. End of story."

"That's all I need to see." I held up my hand. "Does anyone else know about this?"

"Only you, Miss Miko. We're already too far from the station to use my holo-transmitter."

"Oh dear." By that time, I was breathing hard. And I confess for a moment I thought of rushing out and giving Mr. Zump my best karate kick. You know, *Hiiii-YAA!* and all that. Samurai Miko takes out the bad guys.

All by myself.

But that would not do. I couldn't do this alone. And DeeBee had told me we should stick together, like strands.

Except, how could we? The other four AstroKids were back on *CLEO-7*! So I thought and thought and thought. And then I prayed and thought some more. And finally . . .

Someone knocked on the bathroom door.

"Are you all right in there?" asked Assistant Number Two.

"Fine. Be right out."

Had he heard us talking earlier? I wasn't sure. I

was fine. Fine, but running out of time. I turned back to MAC.

"Okay, here's the plan," I whispered. "As soon as I open the bathroom door . . ."

11 Miko's Zillions ✳ ✳ ✳

"Yo, Mr. Z! Pretty cool shuttle!" I gave Donald Zump and his two assistants a thumbs-up. They each sat in front of a different set of controls. A pair of windows gave them a beautiful view ahead into the starry darkness.

But they weren't admiring the view. Their jaws scraped the floor when they saw me.

Oh, but this was perfect. I checked to make sure the good old Face-Lifter was on tight.

"Wa-wa-wait a minute, kid." Mr. Zump found his voice first. "Where did you come from?"

"*CLEO*–7, of course."

Assistant Number One jumped up to grab me, but Mr. Zump pulled back on his arm.

"Don't be crazy," he hissed. "That's Station Commander Chekhov's son!"

Or so it seemed. Because, ha! The other Astro-

Kids still had their face scans stored in the Face-Lifter's memory.

"Just thought I'd come along for the ride." I tried to keep my voice low. "Can somebody give me a tour?"

Mr. Zump nearly melted in his cushy seat. Before he could say no, I turned and walked down the hall.

"You heard the boy, Number One. Give him a tour."

"But—"

But nothing. A minute later, MAC and I had Assistant Number One locked inside a cargo storeroom, way in the back of the ship.

"Yes!" said MAC.

"One down, two to go." I gave MAC a galaxy salute with my pinky.

"Who are you going to be next time?" he asked.

"Let's try . . . Buzz." I touched the emitter button and checked myself in MAC's shiny side. "I think that should work."

Work it did. I can tell you that ten minutes later, we had both assistants and Mr. Zump safely tucked away in the cargo hold.

Hiii-YAH!

"Thanks, MAC. I couldn't have done it without you."

"Or them!" added MAC. "This was a job for all the AstroKids."

Yes, in a way, it had been, thanks to DeeBee's invention and the scanned faces of my friends. I felt for the string in my pocket. It was still there.

That's when it really hit me.

What had we done?

"What do we do now, Miko?" asked MAC.

"A very good question." I gulped. "We'd better figure out a way to turn this ship around, and then . . ."

Thump-thump-thump.

I stopped and turned my head.

"Did you hear that?" I asked MAC.

He twirled, slowly, right there in the middle of the hallway.

And there it was again.

A thumping noise. But it wasn't coming from Mr. Zump and his buddies.

"Over here." MAC floated over to the end of a dark hallway and hovered in front of a small door. "Shall I open it?"

I stared at the door for a second, trying to decide. I should tell you I was a little . . . Well, wouldn't you be scared?

But I had to find out. So I held my breath and tapped the green Open button on the side. And before the door swooshed open all the way, a large stranger tumbled out.

"Are you all right?" I managed to reach out and help the poor man to his feet. He looked as if he had been sleeping in his nice purple suit for a week. Still, right away I could tell he looked just like . . .

"I'm fine, thanks to you." He straightened up and brushed himself off. "My name is Donald Zump."

An Open Chat with Miko Sato's . . . Jaw

Miko's jaw: Hey! How about pulling me back up from the floor, huh?

Miko: Oh, I am sorry. I didn't mean to let you drop that far.

Miko's jaw: Well, now that you've seen the *real* Donald Zump, you can get back to the story.

Honestly, there is not much more story to tell. So I will number it for you for easy reference.

Miko Sato's Three Easy Steps to Finishing Her Story

1. First, we found the real Donald Zump some food to eat. He was starving after almost a week in the water bottle storage closet. He told us thank you at least twenty-four times for rescuing him.

2. Next, we changed course for the real Asteroid A-222, which was way the other direction.

3. Finally, we arrived at my asteroid. Oh, but you should have seen it! Twenty-five restaurants, hundreds of shops, pretty space gardens to walk in, comfy hotels . . . Hundreds and hundreds of shuttles and cargo ships stopped there for a nice meal and a rest. I could hardly believe that I owned the whole thing.

"A little nicer than just a rock in space, eh, Miko?" The *real* Mr. Zump winked at me. The *real* Mr. Zump wasn't anything like the fake Mr. Zump, who was headed for a prison asteroid with Assistant Number One and Assistant Number Two.

The *fake* Mr. Zump looked a lot like the real Mr. Zump. That's why people on *CLEO-7* had believed it was really him. But the real Mr. Zump reminded me of a friendly grandpa. Not that I had ever known my grandpas, but he was the kind of man who made a kid feel comfortable and safe. He would be taking care of A–222 for me. And he helped me figure out a way to send money from the restaurants and shops and stuff back to the Apollo Children's Home. I wanted to help other kids without moms and dads.

"Does this mean you're a zillionaire now, Miko?" asked MAC.

I reached into my pocket for the string that reminded me of my friends back on *CLEO*–7. My *home* back on *CLEO*–7. Our shuttle was headed back in a couple of hours.

I smiled.

"I was rich before I ever had any money, MAC."

RealSpace Debrief

✳ ✳ ✳

Home, Sweet Asteroid

Let's say you want to buy an asteroid. Could you? What is it good for? And how could you tell if you got a genuine asteroid?

Ah, good questions. But let's back up a minute and make sure we know what we're talking about. For instance, are asteroids the same as meteors and meteoroids? What about meteorites and comets? Which is which? It's time for a quick AstroQuiz!

Here's how it works: Match the name (left) with the definition (right). See how many you get right without sneaking a peek at the answers. (Those are upside-down at the bottom of the next page.)

_____ 1. Meteor

_____ 2. Asteroid

_____ 3. Meteorite

_____ 4. Meteoroid

_____ 5. Comet

_____ 6. Shooting Star

_____ 7. Falling Star

a. same as a falling star

b. a piece of meteor that survives to fall to the ground

c. a hunk of ice and frozen rock orbiting the sun

d. the speck of comet or space dust that causes a meteor

e. a light streaking across the night sky, caused by a burning speck of comet or space dust

f. same as a meteor; not actually a star at all

g. a rock smaller than one thousand kilometers across that orbits the sun

SCORE: _____

5–6 — You know your asteroids!

4–5 — Hey, pretty good.

3–4 — One out of two's not bad.

1–2 — Okay, keep reading.

Answers: 1. (e or a) 2. (g) 3. (b) 4. (d) 5. (c) 6. (f, a, or e) 7. (f or e)

So now that you've scored yourself, let's go over the facts. A *meteor* is what you see streaking across the night sky. It's the fireworks that come from a *meteoroid*, which is a little speck of comet or space dust that burns up in the process. Or if the piece is big enough to survive the long fall to the ground, it's called a *meteorite*. (Most meteorites are smaller than a cherry.)

Shooting stars and *falling stars* are just another name for *meteors*, and neither one is a real star. *Comets* are chunks of rock and ice that glob together and orbit the sun. They're changing all the time, depending on how close they get to the heat. We get to see comets every few years when one wanders our way. For instance, a comet named Tempel-Tuttle circles once every thirty-three years. And about every seventy-five years, the famous Halley's Comet zips through our part of the solar system. Its latest visit was in 1986, so we won't be seeing it again for a while, but people have been watching that comet since 240 B.C.

Finally, there are asteroids—now *they're* a lot of fun. Asteroids are basically rocks that orbit the sun, much like tiny planets. You can find most of them in the asteroid belt between Jupiter and Mars, but others are wandering around, too. Perhaps the most famous is called "433 Eros" ("Eros" for short). It's about twenty-one miles long, eight miles wide, and eight miles thick. It's famous because NASA landed a small spacecraft on the surface of the asteroid on February 12, 2001. Nothing like that had ever been done before! The craft took some awesome pictures, which you can see on the Web at *http://near.jhuapl.edu.*

Some asteroids are bigger than Eros. The biggest we know of is called Ceres; it's about 560 miles across. That's about the size of Texas, except that it's in 3-D. Next in size are 10 Hygiea, 4 Vesta, and 2 Pallas, all of which are between 240 and 315 miles across. They're more like the size of Ohio or Utah. Most asteroids are much smaller than states, but there are plenty of rocks out there that are large enough to hold a good-sized resort.

Which brings us back to our first question. Could you buy an asteroid? Well, not at the moment. Of course, you could always "claim" a friendly sized asteroid and make plans to build your own shopping mall on its surface. Just kidding! You still have to wait for a spaceship to take you there.

In the meantime, with all this space stuff flying around the solar system, why don't we get hit on the head more often here on Earth? That's one big difference between Earth and the moon. Look at all the moon's craters, and you see what it's like to be on a place that's not protected. The moon has no atmosphere, no cushion of air around it for protection. Ah, but good old Earth . . . God has created a layer of air around our planet that works just like a shield. And being under God's shield is a very good place to be!

Actually, God's "shield" is more than just air. In fact, the Bible talks about God's shield quite a bit—nineteen times just in the Psalms. Check out Psalm 18:30: "The ways of God are without fault. The Lord's words are pure. He is a shield to those who trust him." When we follow God's ways, we can relax behind His shield, knowing that we are in His care.

Also check out:

- This Web site features interesting stuff from NASA for kids and their parents. It also includes a great "Meteor Glossary." *www.thursdaysclassroom.com/09nov01/corner.html*
- All your asteroid questions answered: *http://spacekids.broaddaylight.com/spacekids/topten_45_0.shtm.*

And the Coded Message Is . . .

$* * *$

You think this AstroKids adventure is over? Not yet! Here's the plan: We'll give you the directions, you find the words. Write them all on a piece of paper. They form a secret message that has to do with *Mid-Air Zillionaire*. If you think you got it right, log on to *www.elmerbooks.org* and follow the instructions there. You'll receive free AstroKids wallpaper for your computer and a sneak peek at the next AstroKids adventure. It's that simple!

WORD 1:
chapter 8, paragraph 2, word 3   _____

WORD 2:
chapter 2, paragraph 49, word 4   _____

WORD 3:
chapter 6, paragraph 12, word 5   _____

WORD 4:
chapter 1, paragraph 3, word 16 _____

WORD 5:
chapter 10, paragraph 39, word 25 _____

WORD 6:
chapter 7, paragraph 4, word 13 _____

WORD 7:
chapter 9, paragraph 6, word 18 _____

WORD 8:
chapter 4, paragraph 14, word 9 _____

WORD 9:
chapter 9, paragraph 3, word 22 _____

(Hint: Miko says to check out Ecclesiastes 4.)

Contact Us! ✳ ✳ ✳

If you have any questions for the author or would just like to say hi, feel free to contact him at Bethany House Publishers, 11400 Hampshire Avenue South, Bloomington, MN 55438, United States of America, EARTH. Please include a self-addressed, stamped envelope if you'd like a reply. Or log on to Robert's intergalactic Web site at *www.elmerbooks.org*.

Launch Countdown

*** ∗ ∗ ∗ ***

AstroKids 10:
Tow-Away Stowaway

Tag is tired of everyone telling him he's too little or too young. No, actually, he's just plain fed up! He wants to be a deep-space pilot, so he spends his afternoons staring out the viewscreen at passing ships. And when an especially interesting ship comes by, he sees his chance for real adventure. "They'll miss me," he thinks. "I'll show them."

So with his trusty friends MAC, the drone, and Zero-G, the dog, he hops on his big sister's space scooter, follows the freighter, and . . . is sucked into the backwash!

Yikes! When the scooter is damaged all he can do is link up to the cargo ship and get inside. But he's in for an unpleasant surprise: It's an unmanned vessel with digital food copiers stuck on the AstroCheesie setting and dozens of drones that simply can't be understood. It doesn't take long before Tag's deep-space adventure turns into a deep-space nightmare, and he knows he's in deep-space trouble. Can Tag ever find his way home?